This EGGcellent book belongs to:

_____

_____

To Fergus, For being incredible and so supportive.
And for Will, My brilliant brother.

NorthParadePublishing

©2015 North Parade Publishing Ltd.
4 North Parade,
Bath BA1 1LF. UK
www.nppbooks.co.uk

The Egg

Written & Illustrated by
Gracie Sandford

Gracie Goose had always done things by herself.

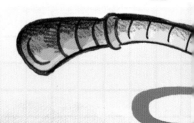

Sometimes she found things
tricky to do because she didn't
have anyone to help her.

But that's how things had
always been for Gracie,
and she didn't want
that to change.

One day, Gracie discovered
something on her travels.
It was an egg!
But where did it come from?
Who did it belong to?

"Well I DON'T want to look after this egg," huffed Gracie. "Someone must be coming back for it." So she snuggled up beside the egg, ready for its owner to return. The dusky day quickly turned into a sleety night.

It was the next day and nobody had come for the egg. Gracie was grumpy. "I don't **WANT** to look after this egg. Not now, **NOT EVER!**" As she grumbled and growled, the egg started to roll away...

...Down into the depths of the sea.

From then on, Gracie tried her
very hardest to keep the egg safe.

"Looking after this egg is hard work,"
sighed Gracie.
"Things were much easier
when I was on my own."

Suddenly,
with a crack and
a crumble,
the egg began to hatch!

Gracie peered down to see a fluffy little bird.
A duckling had hatched from the egg!

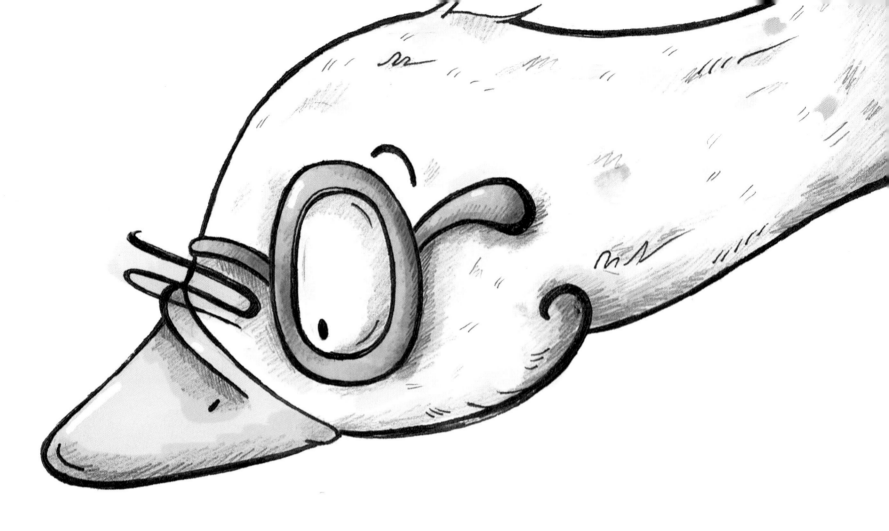

"Wow! You were inside the egg?"
Gracie said.
"Can I call you Egg?"

The duckling nodded
and gave a big quack!

It had been a busy time for Gracie and the goose was tired. Egg held up a blanket for her to sleep under. "This is for me? Nobody has ever given me anything before," smiled Gracie.

From then on
Gracie went
on to have
adventures
with her
new friend.

She had learned that
it wasn't easier doing things alone.
Actually, everything was a lot more
fun with Egg around.